The Kitten Psychologist Collection

THEA VAN DIEPEN

OTHER WORKS

SHORT STORIES AND NOVELLAS
Dreaming Of Her And Other Stories
The Illuminated Heart
The Tree Remembers
Plunged Ashore

THE WHITE CHANGELING SERIES
Hidden In Sealskin (Book 1)
Like Mist Over The Eyes (Book 2)
A Holly Jolly Disaster: Adren And Nadin Try Christmas
(A Silly Christmas Poem)

AN INTERACTIVE STORY
The Tree And The Grave

Find more from the author at
theavandiepen.com/store/

The Kitten Psychologist Collection

THEA VAN DIEPEN

AUSTRALIA

Print ISBN: 978-1-922434-12-8
eBook ISBN: 9798201665418

www.inkprintpress.com

National Library of Australia Cataloguing-in-Publication Data
Van Diepen, Thea
The Kitten Psychologist Collection
58 p.   cm.
ISBN: 978-1-922434-12-8
Inkprint Press, Canberra, Australia
1. Fiction—Animals 2. Fiction—Humorous—General 3. Fiction—Short stories

Summary: When the psychologist acquires a kitten as a client, shenanigans ensue as they work together to negotiate a more equitable world.

First print edition: August 2021
Cover design © Inkprint Press.

The Kitten Psychologist

THERE ONCE WAS A LITTLE KITTEN WHO HAD decided that the outside was bad. One hundred percent, unequivocally, without question or shadow of a doubt, dangerous.

"I mean, why else," said the kitten, purring and cleaning its paws, "would we live in houses?"

But, alas, one day, the kitten's humans took it outside. Carried it right out the door.

"It was terrible," the kitten told me over Skype after the event. "One hundred percent, unequivocally, without question or shadow of a doubt, terrible. There was snow. It was cold and wet and it stuck in my fur. My humans laughed at me when they put me down and I refused to move."

Of course, I thought the kitten was being unreasonable. "Your ancestors lived outside. I'm sure they loved the snow. You should try it again."

"Your ancestors grew crops along the Volga River," the kitten pointed out. "Are you planning on trying that anytime soon?"

Darn kitten had a point.

I tried a different tack. "There's all kinds of things you can do outside that you can't do inside."

"Oh, sure, catch diseases, fall on ice, get attacked by wild animals or drunk drivers, and then die. Although I suppose you could still die inside." It flicked its tail thoughtfully.

"Dying without having ever left your house. That's depressing."

"Fruit flies do it all the time." The kitten's eyes widened. "That *is* depressing."

"See?"

"Then I'll just live a long and healthy life inside and, when I'm dying, I'll have my humans take me outside where I can be with nature and junk. There. Problem solved." The kitten glared at me before being scooted off the desk by its human, who had returned to continue our conversation.

Over the next few days, the kitten would approach the doors and look out windows whenever it thought its humans weren't looking.

But they were. They told me about their kitten's change in behaviour, wondering aloud whether they should let it outside again.

It was at this point they also showed me the YouTube video of their kitten standing indignantly in the snow. I have to admit, it was pretty funny.

Not long after, the kitten called me up on Skype.

"You know, I've been thinking," it said.

"Really? And how did that make you feel?" I adjusted my imaginary spectacles and picked up my imaginary clipboard.

"Shut up. I'm trying to talk." The kitten stuck out its wee pink tongue and I couldn't help but laugh, at which point the kitten glared.

"Sorry, continue."

"I will. As I was saying, I've been thinking. About the outside. At first I was thinking, you know, I'm only a few weeks old. I've got a lot of life left in me. I really could just go out there and try out this whole snow thing again, or I could stay inside for a while. There's lots of time. But then I thought, do I really have as much time as I think? I could die at any moment. The fridge could fall over when I'm trying to open it and squash me, or I could get my tail stuck in an electrical outlet. Someone could be too curious in my vicinity. You know."

I nodded.

"And what if I don't die like that? What if I spend my whole life just staring at the outside instead of prancing out there and just owning it like cats should? What if all I do, for the rest of my life, is wait? I mean, it's not like there's anything stopping me from going outside. There's just... me."

"Sounds like you've made some important progress."

"But what if my humans laugh and take videos of me again?"

I took this moment not to mention that I'd both seen and laughed at the video.

Instead, I gave my most thoughtful face. "So, what you're trying to say is, you would rather go outside without them?"

The kitten stretched before answering. "I'll admit, they're much better as servants than they are as escorts. But they do happen to be able to reach doorknobs. Don't they make doors in more cat-friendly sizes?"

"Yes," I said. *They're called doggy doors,* I thought, but didn't say.

"Excellent." The kitten purred. "I want one. Just for the backyard. I needn't parade myself before the general public just yet."

"I'll mention it to your humans." I suppressed a snigger at the phrase. "I'm sure they'll listen to me."

"Of course they'll listen to you. What else have I been paying you for?" With that, the kitten hung up.

I've really got to tell my friends where their money's been going.

Meh. I can wait until they get their next bank statement.

Behind The Scenes

ONE DAY, IN CONSIDERING WHAT TO WRITE TO MY email list, I had the idea to write about a kitten scared of going outside. Because snow. And dignity.

In true Thea fashion, this wasn't entirely about a kitten.

At the time, I was having a hard time figuring out what I was doing with my life, and resisting stepping out into new things. So. Well. I got to write about myself. As the kitten.

But I also figured, as I have a psychology degree, I could write myself into the story as a psychologist. It didn't quite turn out that way, as I seem to have ended up being in both the psychologist and the kitten and neither of them are exactly me... but it ended up being a rather wonderful therapy session with myself.

It took a bit of thought once I got close enough to the end, with no idea how to conclude it (a common occurrence in, well, any story I write). I sat and stared at the computer screen for a bit, trying to work it out until something slipped into place and there. There it was. The ending. And it was perfect.

The Kitten Psychologist Broaches The Topic Of Economics

There once was a little kitten. No, not the kitten I wrote a story about last time.

Definitely a different kitten.

A very different kitten.

Oh, fine. It's the same kitten.

This kitten had had a hard time going outside. Which is as much to say as it didn't. Not after its first experience with snow, which is probably like a person's first experience with horseradish: you either like it or you don't. And, in this case, the kitten didn't like it.

In the last story, wherein the kitten realized that there was probably maybe some benefit to going outside after paying me good money to sit around and ask it questions containing answers that it decided it had come up with all on its own, I wondered what I was doing with my life being a psychologist to my friends' nine-week-old kitten.

The only problem with this picture (I mean, aside from the obvious) was that the kitten wasn't paying me out of its own money. Let's be serious: I can be a kitten psychologist all I want, but we have to admit that a kitten having its own income stream at nine weeks stretches credibility quite thin.

Which is as much to say as that this kitten had mastered the use of arcane computer enchantments and pulled the money from my friends'—its owners'—bank account.

Frankly, I thought my friends would have figured it out on their own. It might have been a bit cowardly of me to wait until they got a clue and started investigating, but either this kitten was more clever than I thought or my friends had an awful memory for their own spending habits.

I'm not actually sure which was more concerning—but I had plenty of concern on hand to spend no matter which it turned out to be.

In other words, while my friends were out of the country a couple of weeks later, I house-sat. And, as I sat the house, I had a conversation with my friends' kitten.

"You really have to stop this," I said.

"I don't pay you to have an opinion," the kitten said with a swish of its tail.

"You pay me to be a psychologist. That's exactly the same as paying me to have an opinion."

"What happened to unbiased objectivity?"

"Fine. In my unbiased, objective *opinion*, you have to stop this."

The kitten tapped its chin. "Stop what?"

"Paying me from my friends' bank account without their knowledge or consent." As if it didn't already know.

"If you don't like it, I can always find another psychologist…"

"That's not the point."

"And how do you propose I tell them about it when the idea of my sentience is patently absurd to them? Certainly *you* can't. They already think you're crazy."

Obviously, I was going to have to have a conversation with more than just the kitten. "And how would you inform a potential new psychologist of this patently absurd idea?"

"That's different. They're not my human. They aren't used to me. They don't have ingrained habits or ideas about me to contend with."

I bit back a sarcastic remark about the strength of eleven-week-old habits. For the kitten, that was a lifetime. That and it wasn't as if I hadn't had plenty of ingrained habits and ideas of my own about the nature of kittens when this one hired me.

I wondered if maybe I should have kept one or two of them. No amount of income was worth this trouble.

Well. Perhaps not certain amounts of income.

"Well, just give it some thought and see what happens," I finally said.

The kitten avoided me after that.

Which could have been the end of that, I suppose. Certainly it seemed like it, which I was a bit peeved about, to be sure. But, in a few days, I received an email:

Come at once. My humans are away. Sincerely, you know who.

I wondered if the kitten had finally got to my friends' YA collection. That and I went.

"So, I told my humans."

"How did they take it?"

"Now *they're* seeing a psychologist."

"Oh."

Silence.

"You know"—the kitten stretched—"I've come to a realization."

"Oh?"

"This is a ridiculous situation. I'm a kitten. Why do I even need a psychologist?"

I shrugged.

"Exactly. I should be going my wild way on my wild lone. Except..." It glanced at the couch. "...I don't think I'm prepared to give up the amenities of my current living situation."

"Then don't."

"Oh, I'm not. This may not be ancient Egypt, but it's certainly something. Do you suppose you could talk to my humans? Now that I have, that is."

And admit that I'd been complicit in what was essentially theft? Um. "No."

"Drat. I had a feeling this was my fight."

Sure. That's exactly what it was.

"Well, do you have any advice on what I should do next? Some words of wisdom I'll probably ignore when I inevitably come up with something better? Like nothing? I rather like the idea of doing nothing."

"If you'll just come up with something better, then why do you need my advice?"

No, theft was too harsh a word. Underhanded dealing, perhaps?

"It's amusing."

"So, am I psychologist or court jester?"

"Whichever makes you feel better, I suppose." The kitten yawned. "I'm going to have a nap. If you come up with something, email me. Or stop by. I'll pay you as soon as you do."

Who was I kidding? It was definitely theft. By the time I'd gotten home, I realized that. I also realized that, despite the fact that the kitten really should be acting responsibly with its humans, so should I with my friends. With a sigh, I picked up the phone.

I wondered how long I'd be paying them back.

Dear psychologist human,

I'm not entirely sure what you stood to gain by informing my humans of your part in all this. My intention had been for you to merely vouch for my sentience. You have done me a service, and it is right that you should be compensated in turn, not that you should throw that all away.

But no matter. We shall speak when you return from vacation. I think you will see things much more clearly when this is all over.

Sincerely,
You know who.

Behind The Scenes

SOMETIME AFTER SENDING OUT *THE KITTEN PSYCHologist* to my email list, I came back to it, this time for my blog. And I wondered: how on *earth* was a kitten paying a psychologist?

Through immorality, of course.

At which point our psychologist, who could not *not* be aware of what was going on, had to grow a conscience and talk to the kitten about the situation.

To continue the tradition of kittens and psychologists being therapy for me, it turned out that, at the time, I was having issues standing up for myself and saying no to things that weren't good for me. At the same time, I was really unsure about managing money and how to do that effectively, and whether I'd ever make enough money to pay my bills, never mind everything else.

Which, obviously, meant it was time to convince a kitten to remember how to behave in a more... mature fashion. Yes. Let's put it that way.

The Kitten Psychologist vs. The Kitten's Owners

Boy, WAS I IN TROUBLE. I THINK IT would have been worse if I hadn't called my friends the day I left for vacation, which is exactly why I did that. But, man, give them two weeks to steam off and they were still mad.

And, okay, yeah, I deserved it.

When I got back, they demanded an accounting of exactly how much money their kitten had paid me out of their bank account for our sessions and how often. They didn't need to. I'd spent half my vacation angsting about the whole thing and had all my documentation prepared by the time we met in their living room.

This wasn't just some strategy to placate them and get out of trouble. I'd had a lot of time to think during vacation, and I couldn't escape the fact that what I'd done was wrong. For someone who spent a lot of time and energy trying to ignore my conscience when it suited me, it was sure uncomfortable having it yelling at me from three inches away.

Consciences really need to learn a thing or two about personal space.

It also bugged me that I hadn't gotten back to the kitten about its email when it found out what I did.

Fuzzy as it is, that thing can be darn intimidating.

But now I couldn't talk to it. My friends had made sure of that.

"Why would our kitten even need a psychologist?" asked the one with the green shirt. (I may be a coward, but even I know to keep my friends' identities private online. You're welcome, friends.)

"It's sentient. Even humans find that uncomfortable, and we're supposed to be that way."

They didn't appreciate the joke.

"How could you take advantage of it like that?" asked the one in the worn jeans.

Wait, what? "It called me! I had no idea—"

"You could have refused it at any point. Heck, you should have!" Green Shirt fumed. "It's just a kitten, for crying out loud. It doesn't know any better."

"It's a kitten that—" I stopped myself.

Thinking before I spoke was probably a better strategy in this situation if I didn't want it to turn into a warzone. Well, more of one.

"What? A kitten that what?" My friend's eyes had taken on the uncanny appearance of someone aiming a gun.

I cringed.

"Uh. First: yes. I should have refused. I'm sorry I didn't, which is why I called you in the first place. Second: you didn't know your kitten was sentient until just over two weeks ago. How do you know it's not capable of seeing the right and wrong of its actions for itself?"

"It's a kitten!" exclaimed Worn Jeans.

"More than that, it's a cat," said Green Shirt. "Cats aren't exactly known for their strong grasp on morality."

"Well, they do know what it is," amended Worn Jeans. "They just don't follow it. On purpose. So, in the case of our kitten…"

"Cats will be cats?" I supplied.

They nodded.

"And, since your kitten is now too young to know these things, and will grow up not to follow them anyways, it's up to us to make all of its moral decisions for it?"

"As much as possible, yes," said Worn Jeans. "We do know we can't be there all the time in every situation."

"Which is why it's so important that we only let it be with people that are committed to the same thing, and not boneheads like you," Green Shirt said, arms crossed.

"Boneheads?" said Worn Jeans. "That's a little harsh."

"Well, it's true!"

I fidgeted. "Should I leave?"

"That depends. Are you going to *leave* leave, or go talk to the kitten again?"

"Well, see, it sent me an email that I haven't responded to yet…"

"It has an email address?" asked Worn Jeans in bewilderment.

"And a Tumblr, too." I pulled out my phone.

The kitten's latest post was a picture of a fall forest, with the caption 'We are more than we feel'.

The previous was a sepia-filtered photo of latte art.

"It has a hipster blog?" said Worn Jeans.

Green Shirt grabbed my phone. "I'm not sure how to process this." Green Shirt's eyes were concerningly wide. "Is that latte telling me to live my dreams?"

"Maybe you should, uh, get to know your kitten better?" I suggested. "And, meanwhile, we can work on a payment plan for me?"

"Yeah," said Green Shirt, still scrolling through the kitten's Tumblr. "But, uh, I'm beginning to see why it needed a psychologist."

That sounded hopeful. I swear my bank account perked up at it.

And, if I wasn't still having an attack of conscience, that would have been that. "You know, I think your kitten is plenty able to do what's right.

Enough that making those decisions for it is only going stop it from wanting to."

Damn, damn, damn.

I knew from their expressions that that had been the absolute worst thing to say.

Green Shirt handed me back my phone. "I think we understand our kitten better than you do. We'll work out a payment plan, but we're not budging on our requirements for your behaviour with it."

"Or we can just pretend I never said that."

"Really?" said Worn Jeans.

I gulped.

"I can't believe you." At which point my friend upped and left the room.

This is what I get for being a psychologist to a kitten. Correction: for being desperate enough to be a psychologist to a kitten.

"We'll, uh, work it out over email," I said as I high-tailed it out of there before Green Shirt could do anything.

So, that was finally that. Years of friendship hanging precariously in the balance all because we disagreed about what their kitten could and could not handle.

It's one of those moments where you'd like to laugh over the ridiculousness of it, but it was a little too serious for that.

I mean, we'd have never been in this situation if I hadn't let the kitten take advantage of them.

But wouldn't that mean that the kitten would have always been stuck? Aren't I doing it a favour by standing up for it to my friends?

I don't know.

Morality is hard, guys.

Dear psychologist human,

I cannot believe you showed my humans my tumblr. Do you not understand that it was meant to be ironic? They think it's serious!

On another note: You still have not responded to my previous email. This displeases me. I require that you respond in a timely manner.

We must speak.

Sincerely,
You know who.

Behind The Scenes

So. Readers of this series by this point had only had to deal with the kitten and the psychologist. And, this being told through first person, it was easy to keep the two separate without ever having to reveal gender.

Why didn't I want to reveal gender?

Because I thought it would be interesting to write without specifying gender.

Which is fun... until you double the number of characters in your series and then have to come up with ways of referring to them and also personalities for them that are distinct without being stereotypical such that people give them genders that aren't included in the text.

While figuring that out, I was also working through the dynamic of some, well, let's say interesting perspectives. At the time, I was having a hard time working out who I wanted to be and how I wanted to act without feeling trapped into patterns formed from other people's perceptions of me (or, at least, what I thought those perceptions were, which is an important distinction).

With the psychologist trying to act in a way that would soothe a sore conscience, the kitten being pushed towards independence, and the owners very confused as to why the status quo ever needed changing, I had enough angles to keep myself occupied as I tried to write my way to a conclusion.

The Kitten Psychologist Tries To Be Patient Through Email

DEAR KITTEN,

I would absolutely love to speak with you, but your humans, as you say, have decided I can't ever see you. You'll have to deal with the Tumblr thing on your own.

Sincerely,
Your psychologist

Dear psychologist human,

There is no reason to be rude with me. As you see perfectly well, we can talk through email. Your payment will be minimal to none as a result, but I still need your help, so you are still my psychologist.

My current dilemma has less to do with Tumblr and more to do with the conversation you had with my humans. I overheard you, you know. What is this nonsense about cats not being moral? We are most certainly moral. Explain this to me.

I also seem to be having difficulties accessing my humans' bank account. Do you have any solutions to that?

Sincerely,
You know who

Dear kitten,

That's... not really how being a psychologist works. It's a job. I need to get paid.

And, while I disagree with your owners on principle, your last paragraph sort of proves their point.

Sincerely,
Your psychologist

Dear psychologist human,

Thank you for Skyping with me again. Finally. I hope you now understand the unfeasibility of my obtaining employment (not to mention a bank account of my own) in order to pay you. This really isn't a moral matter so much as a pragmatic one.

I am a kitten. And I live in a world where kittens cannot get jobs. I, therefore, cannot get paid. You will have to help me, regardless.

Meanwhile, I've noticed my humans are more attentive to me of late. Not in the way I like. They have been keeping me from doing as I please in regards to electronics and leaving the house.

Speaking to them about the matter has changed nothing.

How do I convince them that I am perfectly capable and trustworthy enough to be left on my own?

Sincerely,
You know who

Dear kitten,

If you're actually going to take any advice I give, you're going to pay me. Or work something else out. Otherwise, you're telling me that you're not trustworthy and that working for you isn't working for you. It's you using me.

Which, while I'm being perfectly honest with you, is what you've been doing with your owners.

Sincerely,
Your psychologist

Dammit. Maybe I shouldn't have worded that so strongly, but I'd sent it before I could stop myself. I'd been emailing my friends, too. They wanted to know how to deal with their kitten, and I'd agreed to give them free sessions in exchange for keeping the money the kitten had paid me from their bank account.

It was one of those things you know is a bad idea, but you're too worried about what might happen if you don't that you say yes to it anyways.

Those sessions were... hard. They're my friends, but I had to be their psychologist instead and, let me tell you, telling your friends to solve their own problems doesn't ever go over very well. Especially when they're dead set against it. All they wanted to do was figure out what to do to get the kitten to do what they wanted. All I wanted was to get them out of my office before I yelled at them.

I freak out over my finances too much. If I hadn't, I never would have been in this situation. Now, if I could just get a time machine and go tell my past self that, that would be great.

Oh. A new email. Great.

Dear psychologist human,

And how, exactly, do you propose I "work something else out"?

Sincerely,
You know who

I could always turn off my computer and pretend I hadn't read that. Or that my email had glitched and I'd never received the message.

Except that I'm doing that thing where I'm trying to get out of this darn mess.

Dear kitten,

Talk to your owners about it. And don't let them tell you you're not able to do anything. The moment you're feeling helpless or powerless or incapable is the moment you've started going in the wrong direction.

Sincerely,
Your psychologist

Dear psychologist human,

I am never helpless, powerless, or incapable. I am a feline. But I will speak to them, since you obviously didn't know what you meant in the first place.

Sincerely,
You know who

I'm never going to get over getting emails from a kitten that's basically telling me it's Voldemort. It's certainly mean enough to be him.

I wrote an angry reply which I deleted right afterwards as I sat back in my chair and sighed.

Seven or so additional deleted angry replies later, another email arrived in my inbox. Two emails, actually.

Dear psychologist human,

You have a devious mind. I like you.

Sincerely,
You know who

And then, from my friends:

You're not going to believe what our kitten just did. Can we have our next session earlier in the week?

I'm not sure what to feel about this.
…
I'm really not sure what to feel about this.

To my friends:

I'm open on Wednesday between 3pm and 5pm. Does that work for you?

It's amazing what you can do on autopilot.

From my friends:

Yes, 3pm. This can't wait.

Uh oh. What did the kitten go and do now?
And how am I going to get out of this with my skin intact?

Behind The Scenes

WHILE EPISTOLARY NOVELS HAVE YET TO MAKE IT TO my bibliography, I figured it would be *hilarious* to write this as a series of emails between the psychologist and kitten. After all, *The Kitten Psychologist vs the Kitten's Owners* had ended with an email. And, well, I figured readers would have read enough to be able to fill in the blanks. Like an inside joke. In the middle of a series. Which had basically been a series of therapy sessions for me.

Oh boy.

I had also hoped that this series would be brought to an end, say, a story ago, and it became increasingly clear as I wrote this one that I had at least one more instalment to go. But how would it end? I was already trying to write to an ending I knew nothing about, since I hadn't planned this series *at all* aside from, "Ha ha, wouldn't it be fun to write about a kitten with a psychologist?", and since I was simultaneously working through my own life problems through the writing of these stories.

You can't really plan endings when you're being your own psychologist. You either get there, or you stop.

So I sat down, wrote to the end, and hoped like heck that I would find the end soon.

The Kitten Psychologist And What The Kitten Did

WEDNESDAY ARRIVED, AND 2:55PM found me in my office, sweating.

I've really got to turn the heat down in this place.

Oh.

It was down.

Well, crap.

I'd cancelled my other appointments that day when it became clear partway through my *first* one that all I could think about was *this* one. This one in thirty minutes.

My lunch tried to regurgitate itself. It did an excellent job.

4 out of 5 carrot-flavoured lumps for effort.

Who knew a kitten would be so much trouble?

…I did.

And I went for it anyways.

And now I'm here.

Was the thermostat actually working, or just pretending to work?

I simultaneously wished the kitten's owners would come early, and that they'd never come at all. Between ripping this experience off like a bandaid and waking up to find it all a dream... I honestly didn't know which one would be better.

Maybe the bandaid.

I sighed.

Yeah, it was the bandaid.

2:57.

What if I didn't show up? I could escape out the window, right? Three stories wouldn't be hard to climb down. I was sure it wouldn't be.

2:58.

My knee bobbed like a squirrel on cocaine. When had that started? *Stop that. Stop it.* Gah. Now the other one was doing it.

2:58.

Still?

Agh.

Okay, this is ridiculous. Pull yourself together. Or at least pretend to.

The door opened.

I jumped.

The kitten entered first, followed by Worn Jeans and Green Shirt.

Oh dear lord.

I licked my lips. Had I had enough to drink today? My mouth was undergoing desertification.

"Hello," I said. Cleared my throat.

"Tell the psychologist what you told us," Worn Jeans demanded of the kitten.

'The psychologist.' Ouch.

"I went to the bank," the kitten said as it leapt onto my desk and sat primly, wrapping it tail around itself.

I blinked. "You what?"

"We've obviously got to supervise it more," said Worn Jeans, arms crossed.

"Wait, wait," I said, holding up my hands. "Two months ago, your kitten was too afraid to go outside. Period."

"It was?" asked Green Shirt. "I didn't know that."

Both of my friends had been sitting tensely and, due to my nerves, I hadn't noticed until now as they both... softened? Not much, but enough to remind me to listen. To focus.

I took a deep breath.

"Well, I'm not now," said the kitten. "Obviously." Its usual arrogance faltered for a split second when it glanced at its owners, but it soon regained its composure. "Since the source of all our arguments seems to be money and how to get it, it followed that I should start by opening a bank account. However I end up acquiring money, I must have some place to put it first. And let us not forget that this all started because I was paying you out of an account not my own. It was the logical course of action."

Never mind Voldemort. Now I was dealing with Spock. Or Spocklemort? Voldepock? "So you have an account now."

"Of course not. The idiot banker refused to open one for me."

"Because you're a cat."

"Because I have no money. And I'm underage." The kitten scoffed. "Underage. The whole system's felinist. I needed to be accompanied by a parent or guardian, apparently. Which my humans refuse to do for me. Neither will they lend me any money with which to make my first deposit."

I raised an eyebrow. "Can you blame them?"

The kitten eyed its owners. "I suppose not. But still. I'm trying to be responsible, here. You would think they'd see that."

"And how are you supposed to pay back your loan, exactly?" asked Worn Jeans.

"I'm working on that!" the kitten retorted.

I made what I hoped was a placating gesture to both of them. "I'm confused. Why are you talking to me about this?"

"Don't you see?" Worn Jeans' hands jabbed the air. "It went to the bank. On its own."

"Why is this even a problem?" Green Shirt exploded.

What the what now?

The kitten and I exchanged glances, but said nothing.

"Honey…" Worn Jeans said.

"No, really," Green Shirt continued, "why do we need to make a big deal about this? So it went to the bank to open an account. That's not a crime."

Worn Jeans scowled. "And whose money will it fill that account with? Ours?"

The kitten flicked its tail.

"It's going to pay us back. It said it would."

"It stole money from us for weeks, why would we believe what it said? And why does a kitten need money?"

"Because your friend needed help!" the kitten yelled.

Oh. Well. That changes things a bit.

Behind The Scenes

THE SERIES SAT FOR A COUPLE YEARS AFTER THE previous instalment. Chilling. Unfinished. Frustrating. I'd ended it on a cliffhanger and had absolutely no idea what happened next, only that the kitten had done something that was, I assumed, egregious.

And it sat not because I couldn't come up with ideas of how to continue. I had plenty of them. Many were awful, true, but plenty nonetheless. The problem was that, when I sat down to write, writing didn't happen. I couldn't seem to get my fingers to do the thing.

Until one day, the switch flipped and I found myself sitting in front of my computer, able to write again.

My current working theory is that trying to write this part earlier had been me forcing something to happen that wasn't ready yet. Like I had to process some stuff before I'd be able to sit in on my next therapy session with me and my writing.

When I could finally write it, I didn't realize what had changed, but in re-reading the story to write about how I wrote it, I figured it out.

I needed a new perspective on what I'd been looking at for so long. I needed to allow the characters to have layers. To have hidden things.

I'd gone into these stories thinking it would help me solve what I was working through by giving me something new, or changing something that wasn't working for me. And while I started this instalment of the series thinking that I would be going down those same lines again, some part of me was finally ready to see that I already had what I needed. Hidden, but ready to be revealed.

And it was time to admit that it was there.

The Kitten Psychologist And The Kitten Come To A Conclusion

BOTH WORN JEANS AND GREEN SHIRT looked at me.

"Well, I have been having a hard time getting patients." I said. "How did you know?"

"You told me about it. Before you knew I was sentient. And you'd told everyone else about it just before then, if not so bluntly as you did me." The kitten glared at its owners. "What else did you think all those tales of financial woe were about? So, since you nodded and listened and did nothing to help, I decided to do so. After all, I had problems, and here was a psychologist in need of patients. You would have paid for the sessions if it had been your idea."

I vaguely recalled that day—it had been at a party. Unfortunately, I'd been so down I'd had a little too much to drink to remember details.

"So you do have a heart," I said. My friends bristled, but the kitten gave me a wry smile.

"I wasn't about to let you know that. I am a cat. But," it sighed, "it appears circumstances have forced me to reveal myself. Don't go telling anyone."

"I'd thought you were just being down on yourself," Worn Jeans said to me.

"How are you paying for this office?" Green Shirt asked.

"Weren't we here to talk about..." I waved my hands in their general vicinity. To tell the truth, I was embarrassed to admit that the only way I'd been able to afford the office for the past year or so was by subsisting off of less-than-stellar food. Which hadn't helped my emotional state, that was for sure. "Was this only about the bank, or is there more?"

"Well, clearly there's more," remarked Worn Jeans.

And then proceeded to say nothing more.

"Ah, yes, well." The kitten cleared its throat. "I went to more than the bank."

"You what?" said both my friends in aghast chorus.

The kitten ignored them and addressed me instead. "Have you heard of the cat cafe that opened up in our neighbourhood?"

"The Cat's Paws?"

"Take a Paws. Yes. They're... willing to give me a job. If I have a bank account so they can deposit my pay-cheques."

My friends and I all sat back. Hadn't the kitten lectured me at length about the unfeasibility of kittens getting jobs? In great detail? Over Skype and email? Without giving me a chance to say much more than three words in a row?

"What will you be doing?" asked Green Shirt.

"Roaming their establishment, entertaining their customers by virtue of being feline. In return, they would provide me the means with which to pay off the debt I have incurred and, afterwards, continue to make use of this fine psychologist's knowledge and experience."

"Provided everything you do is your idea," I said, a little dazed at being called a fine psychologist.

"Precisely. I do have my dignity to maintain."

"And that's why you went to the bank," said Worn Jeans, as though not quite sure to believe these words.

The kitten nodded.

"You did all of this to help our friend?" asked Green Shirt.

Oh. Wow. I hadn't even thought of that.

"A friend who did everything possible to help all of us when my first strategy fell apart."

"So what do we do now?" asked Green Shirt, but not of me. Of the kitten.

Worn Jeans had also turned away from me and to the young cat.

The kitten, in turn, drew back and gave me a pleading stare.

Be honest, I mouthed.

The kitten's head drooped, but only for a moment. It took a breath, drew itself up, and said, with the kind of poise only a cat can have: "I cannot do this by myself. Will you help me?"

Maybe one day, the kitten won't need a psychologist. Maybe one day, I won't need a kitten. That's what I'd thought more times than I could count ever since I decided to grow a conscience.

But, before I left my office on Wednesday with my friendships intact and the kitten, impatient, already gone outside, I paused a minute with Worn Jeans and Green Shirt.

"It's hard to think it was scared of going outside when it first spoke with you," said Worn Jeans. "I wish we'd known, but it looks like you really helped."

I guess I did.

"Will our kitten's visits be enough to help you keep afloat?"

"Not really, but it's better than nothing."

"Anything we can do?" asked Green Shirt.

I considered.

Referrals would be great, but how awkward was it to tell your friends to go to a psychologist?

Probably no more awkward than telling them their cat was sentient.

"Let your kitten make its own choices," I said. "And if you hear of anyone needing a psychologist, send them my way."

"What if those people include us?" asked Worn Jeans.

"Just make sure you pay me," I said, with a bit of a forced chuckle. My friends smiled, but I remembered our previous sessions. "How about, for now, let's focus on being friends for a while. I've been moping around by myself long enough."

"Sounds good to me," said Worn Jeans. "Want to come over for dinner tomorrow?"

"That sounds amazing. I've… uh… been having a lot of Kraft Dinner lately." I paused. Did I want to leave the reason in the blanks for them to fill in? But I supposed that, for all the talking we'd done, it was the things we hadn't said that had led to all this trouble in the first place. "For the last year, actually. That's how long my finances have been this tight."

"Then," said Green Shirt, putting a hand on my shoulder. "Come over as often as you like."

There once was a little kitten who had decided that the outside was bad. One hundred percent, unequivocally, without question or shadow of a doubt dangerous. And yet, one day, outside it went.

Now the time had come for its psychologist to go outside, too.

And, once my friends and the kitten had left the building, that's exactly what I did.

Behind The Scenes

As I was writing what I knew was the last part of this story, I felt this nudge to go back to the beginning. Why did the kitten need help to begin with? What good had that done, both for the kitten and the psychologist? And how did those initial circumstances tie in with the ending, anyways?

The thing about writing what you thought would be a silly one-off, and then deciding later you'd write a series, means that the whole thing feels so... random. I'd worried whether the first part of the story even made sense as part of the series, or if it was this odd part, hanging out with the rest so their existence could be justified.

So, as the bomb of the kitten having a conscience had dropped and the aftermath played out, I was taking a whole new look at what had really happened leading up to and during that kitten's first session with the psychologist.

Because if this had happened that way, then really... really.

And then I found the first lines of the story going through my head again, and I understood.

The story had never been about the kitten.

It had been about the psychologist.

I'd started writing these stories with the psychologist as a humorous, semi self-insert, to help this kitten through the problem I'd personally been having with stepping out. And, as it turns out, when you write a series of stories as therapy sessions for yourself, the story's not over until the character you've really based on yourself gets the help you've been needing.

Funny how that works.

(P.S. I really want a cat cafe called Take a Paws to be a thing irl. Someone, go do that.)

About The Author

THEA VAN DIEPEN spent the first ten years of her life on a tree-wrapped acreage where an inquisitive child might believe in magic. Nowadays, she lives in Edmonton, breathing life into stories in the form of books such as the *White Changeling* series, a web-comic, and a video game.

Her website is theavandiepen.com, where she can be contacted in English and French... so long as you don't ask her to count in French, as she tends to miss numbers ending in six entirely by accident.

More By Thea van Diepen

DREAMING OF HER AND OTHER STORIES

A short story collection

From the story 'Glass'

Why can't they see what I see? For some irrational reason, Isabelle felt she would be unable to go to sleep until she could answer that question.

"Go away," she told it, hoping that, by doing so, she could ignore the problem. She tried to turn her mind to sleep, to her drawing, to something that would not take hold of her mind in the way this question was. Instead, Isabelle found those seven words growing in her mind, disturbing her attempted self-distraction. It seemed incomprehensible that she and her mother could look at the very same thing, and yet see it in so completely different ways. They both had eyes that worked, they both wore glasses, the world should look no different to them. Even if they switched glasses—

A wild thought entered Isabelle's mind and, without a word, she left her room, tiptoeing down the hall to her parent's bedroom.

Grab your copy now to keep reading!

https://payhip.com/b/xEyg